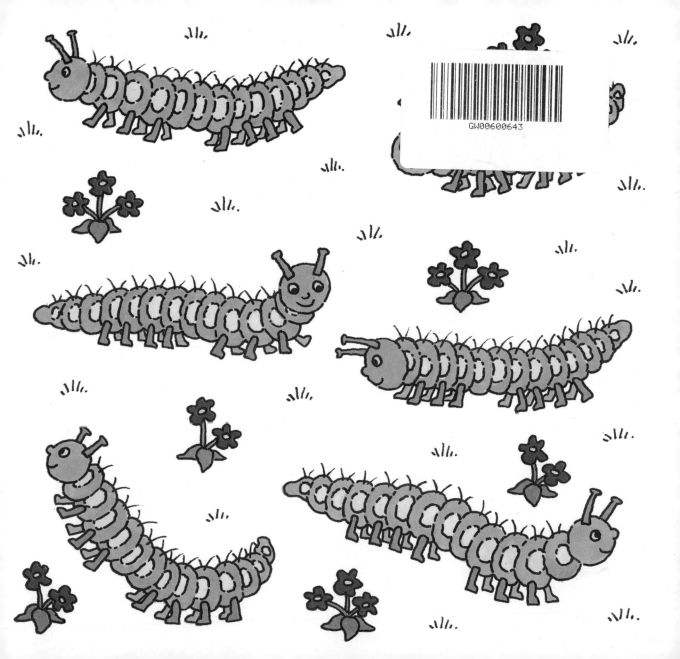
GW00600643

Nanette Newman was born in Northampton and studied at the Royal Academy of Dramatic Art. She has starred in many films, plays and television series. She has also written many books, a lot of them for children. Nanette and her husband, author and film director Bryan Forbes, live in Surrey with their daughters, Sarah and Emma.

Susie Lacome was born in London but grew up in Scotland and trained to be an illustrator at Edinburgh College of Art. She has illustrated many children's books and is married to an illustrator. They share a large Edinburgh studio with two very young budding artists – their children, Rachel and Matthew!

British Library Cataloguing in Publication Data
Newman, Nanette
    Charlie the noisy caterpillar
    I. Title   II. Lacome, Susie
    823'.914[J]
    ISBN 0-7214-9597-4

First edition
Published by Ladybird Books Ltd Loughborough Leicestershire UK
Ladybird Books Inc Auburn Maine 04210 USA
© BRYAN FORBES LTD MCMLXXXIX
© LADYBIRD BOOKS LTD MCMLXXXIX
All rights reserved. No part of this publication may be reproduced, stored in a retrieval system, or transmitted in any form or by any means, electronic, mechanical, photo-copying, recording or otherwise, without the prior consent of the copyright owners.
Printed in England

CHARLIE
THE NOISY CATERPILLAR

by NANETTE NEWMAN
illustrated by SUSIE LACOME

Ladybird Books

When Charlie the caterpillar hatched out of his egg, his mother thought he was the most beautiful baby she had ever seen.

Whenever friends came to visit, she would show him off
proudly and say, 'He's the best little caterpillar in the whole
world.'

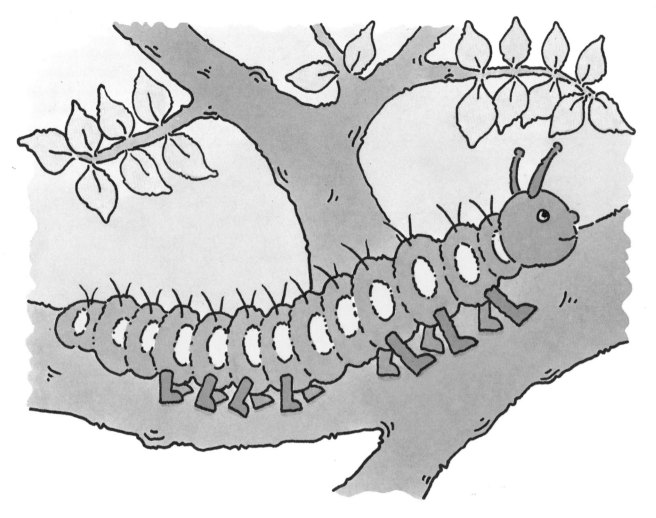

Now even though caterpillars have lots of feet, they are usually as quiet as quiet can be. But not Charlie. As he grew bigger and bigger, he also grew noisier and noisier.

'Shush, Charlie!' his mother would say twenty times a day. But when Charlie ran out to play, his feet made him sound more like an elephant than a baby caterpillar.

And when Charlie started school, his teacher said, 'I'm afraid it's impossible to teach the other children with all the noise that Charlie makes. You'd better take him home.'

On the way home Charlie and his mother passed the wise owl sitting on his favourite branch.

'Whooooo's making that dreadful noise?' asked the owl. 'It woke me up.'

'It's just Charlie,' Charlie's mother said with a sigh. 'He'll try not to do it again.'

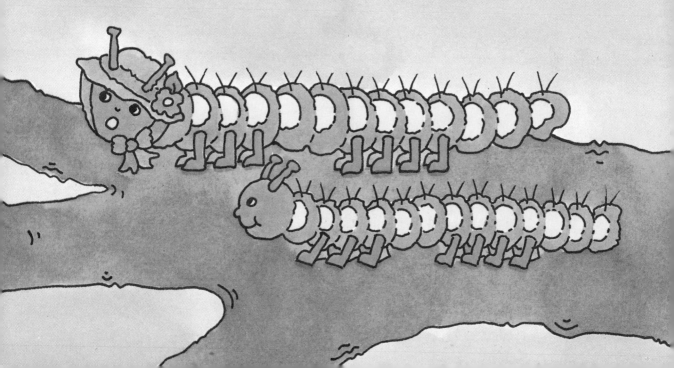

But as Charlie grew bigger, the sound of his feet crashing along branches of trees or the stems of plants grew even louder. Neighbours began to complain.

Charlie's mother didn't know what to do. 'Wrap his feet in cobwebs,' suggested the spider who lived next door.

So Charlie's mother spent all day gathering cobwebs, and when she had enough, she wrapped each one of Charlie's feet in them. It took hours, but finally Charlie slithered away without a sound.

But she hadn't even finished tidying up when she heard the sound of heavy footsteps. Charlie poked his nose through the door. 'The wind blew the cobwebs away,' he said sadly.

As the weeks went by, Charlie stayed at home more and more. He was tired of everyone telling him to stop making so much noise. Then one day Charlie had an idea. He went off to see the wise owl.

At first the owl wasn't at all pleased to see him. 'You woke me out of a very sound sleep,' he said crossly.

'Waking people up is the only thing I seem to be any good at,' said Charlie.

'Trooooo,' said the owl.

'Well, I know you oversleep sometimes and it makes you cross,' said Charlie. 'Perhaps you'd like me to wake you up every night to make sure you don't miss anything.'

The owl looked at him for a minute. 'Charlie, that's a wonderful idea!' he exclaimed. 'I do have trouble waking up. It would be great to have someone to help me.

'The butterflies need to know when to fly away.

'And I bet you could wake up the squirrels after their winter rest, and the cats are always napping... Why, I'm sure lots of animals would be glad if you woke them up.'

So now Charlie is very happy. He loves his job and there is always someone who needs him to wake them up. After all, there aren't many noisy caterpillars around!

No one ever complains about Charlie's noisy feet, and his mother is very proud of him, too.

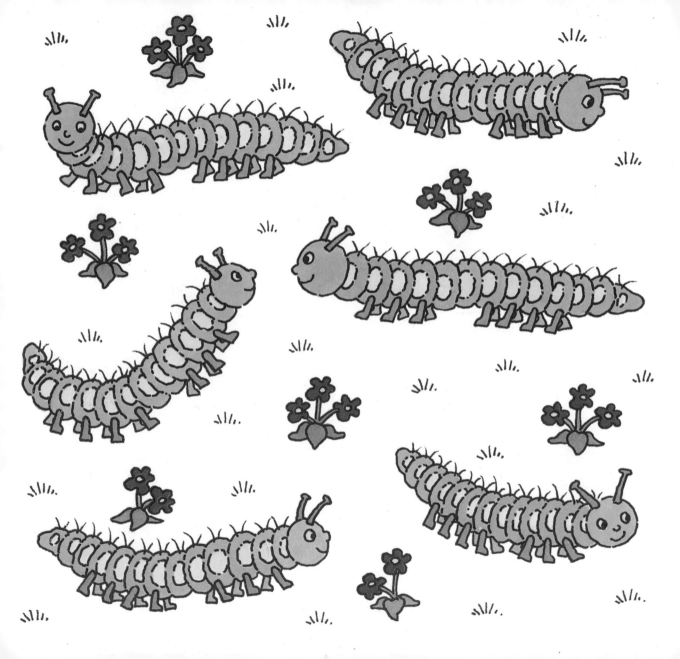